GREECE!
ROME!
MONSTERS!

John Harris

illustrations by
CALEF BROWN

The J. Paul Getty Museum
Los Angeles

Table of

MONSTERS —————

minotaur

Pan

Pegasus

Phoenix

Salamander

Scylla and Charybdis

Sirens

Sphinx

Unicorn

WARNING!

The ancient world—Greece and Rome, to be more exact—
had tons and tons of monsters running around.
Or at least they thought they did.

These monsters are found in Greek and Roman mythology—
fairy tale-type stories that are still big today.
They show up in books and poems,
in paintings, as sculptures—they're everywhere.

Here's a bunch of these creepy creatures.
Read on if you dare!

Basilisk

One look from him
and *whammo!*—you're dead.
That's a basilisk for you.
(And that's where we get the strange expression *a basilisk gaze.*)

A basilisk was basically a snake, but a snake with a difference:
it had the head, feet, and wings of a rooster and the tail of a dragon.
(How's this for gross? If you were stung by a basilisk,
your flesh would fall off your bones!)
A basilisk often has a crown-y thing on its head.
Here comes His Royal Highness, The Basilisk!
Run for your life!

CENTAUR

A creature that was half man, half horse.
    (The upper half was the man part, thank goodness.)
Centaurs were pretty wild: ancient "party animals,"
    you might say—
        though one of them, named Chiron,
            was way different and became famous
        for his great wisdom and goodness.

CERBERUS

Three-headed watchdog who guarded
the entrance to the gloomy realm known as Hades
(some call it the Underworld).
Extremely scary.

Cerberus would let the spirits of the dead IN,
but he certainly didn't let them OUT
(which meant he was someone you didn't want
to meet for a long, long, long time).

Cerberus had a run-in with the hero Hercules,
and he's also part of the sad story
of the singer named Orpheus,
who managed to sneak past him.
But they were exceptions to the rule,
the rule being:
Don't mess with Cerberus.

CHIMaERA

The Chimaera breathed fire—*out of a lion's mouth!*
As if that wasn't bad enough,
the Chimaera had a goat's head coming up out of the middle of her
back and, for a tail, a hissing snake. *Whoa!*
    The only person who could get rid of this major nuisance
    was the hero Bellerophon, who managed to do so
    with the help of his beautiful winged horse, Pegasus.

The Chimaera was so way out
that she gave her name (spelled a little differently)
to any fantastic dream.
    Are you chasing after a chimera?
If so—you're not going to catch it!

CYCLOPS

A very violent, huge guy
with only one eye in the middle of his forehead.
There were actually a lot of Cyclopes stomping around,
snacking on unlucky humans.
But the most famous one was named Polyphemus,
and he had a very unpleasant run-in
with the clever Greek hero Odysseus
and ended up with no eye at all—*ouch!*
A rotten trick, but somebody had to do it.

GRIFFIN

The griffin was a major, major monster in the ancient world.
Griffins took different shapes,
but your basic griffin had the head of a bird
   (a big, scary bird, like a falcon or eagle)
   with the appropriate wings,
   only they were sticking out from the body of a lion.
      For some weird reason,
      griffins are often shown with pointy ears, too.

Griffins pop up everywhere: people in the
ancient world couldn't get enough of them.
You'll find them on rings, coins, pots, carvings,
and of course in the form of stone statues.
   They were often carved on tombs
   because they were so frightening that they could
   protect the tomb from bad people or other monsters,
   who were too scared to come close.

For obvious reasons,
they are sometimes shown flying.
      Duck, it's a griffin!

HARPIES

If you've heard the word *harpy*,
it's probably been used to describe a woman who nags a lot.
But in ancient times, a Harpy was an evil demon,
part woman, part bird.

They were noisy, dirty, and dangerous.
REALLY dirty and dangerous.

The main Harpy story goes like this:
An old guy named Phineus had done something
to make Zeus, the king of the gods, mad.
So Zeus decided to punish Phineus
in a particularly nasty way:
every time Phineus started to eat,
the Harpies would swoop down
and, well, make a mess in his food.
Result: a very skinny Phineus.

After a while, two sons of the North Wind
took pity on the old man and
chased the squawking, smelly
Harpies away, permanently.

Let's hear it for the
two sons of the North Wind!

HiPPOCaMP

No, silly, this is not a camp for hippos …
In point of fact, a hippocamp was a sea creature,
        half horse and half fish.
Sometimes you'll see a picture of a hippocamp
pulling the chariot of Poseidon, god of the sea.

Giddy-up, hippocamp!

MANTICORE

You wouldn't want to run into a manticore.
It had: the body of a lion
and the head of a man
    with three rows of teeth (upper and lower)
      and a long tail with poison-tipped spines at the end.

    Yikes! If a manticore didn't bite you to death,
    he'd tear you up with that tail…
            Definitely nightmare material.

Medusa

The three Gorgon sisters were winged, serpent-haired
monsters with really sharp claws.
The very famous Medusa
    got an even rawer deal than her siblings:
she was the only Gorgon who could be killed, which Perseus,
    the great hero, proceeded to do by looking at her reflection
    (*not at HER*) in his polished shield.
        (If he'd looked at HER, he'd have been turned to stone,
        just like everyone else.)
But Perseus was one cagey customer—as Medusa discovered.
She hissed, she flew around with those claws
    ready to rip Perseus to shreds,
    she tried every trick in the book,
    but by the end of the day Medusa—*chop! chop!*—
        no longer had a head.

MINOTAUR

A beast, half man, half bull.

The Minotaur lived in the famous Labyrinth. Built by King Minos, the Labyrinth was a really confusing maze that you couldn't find your way out of before the Minotaur found you and ate you.

Every year poor, innocent young people were sent into the Labyrinth, never to be seen again. This kept the Minotaur happy, and when the Minotaur was happy, King Minos was happy.

One year, the hero Theseus was among the young people sent into the Labyrinth. Bad news for the Minotaur! Theseus was clever and strong, and he ended up KILLING the beast. *Wow!*

But then he had to get OUT.

Fortunately for Theseus, a girl named Ariadne—who was in love with him—gave him a l-o-o-o-o-o-n-g piece of string and told him to let it trail behind him so that he could later follow it back to the beginning. Theseus took Ariadne's advice, and that's how he escaped.

King Minos was really mad about this, but what could he do?

Not much.

The major Spanish artist Pablo Picasso would later paint many pictures of the Minotaur stalking around.

PaN

A faun was a merry beast with little horns on his head and pointy ears—
half human, half goat—associated with spooky forest sounds.
(In Greece, fauns went by the name of "satyrs.")

Mischievous without really being evil,
fauns liked to dance and prance around having fun.
    You usually see them laughing,
    playing hide-and-seek in the woods; whatever.
    (The French composer Claude Debussy wrote a famous piece
        about a daydreaming faun. Typical!)

If you see only ONE faun, the faun you see is probably going to be Pan.

      Pan was the god of sheep and shepherds.
    You often see pictures of him playing on his reed pipes—
    panpipes, get it!—which he invented, no less.

      Pan, like most fauns, was a little on the wild side
      and liked to jump out from behind a bush or rock
        and scare people—*Booo!*—
        which produced that sudden
        creepy feeling we call *panic*.
        Yep: that's where the word comes from.

PEGASUS

A horse that could fly through the air on big white wings.
If there's a more beautiful idea going, I don't know what it might be.

Pegasus was said to have sprung up from the head of Medusa
when her head was cut off—*eew!*
(See the story of Medusa, a few pages back.)
Pegasus was so cool: when his hoof touched the earth,
a magical spring burst out of the ground.

The only person who could ride Pegasus
was the great hero Bellerophon.
Together, Bellerophon and Pegasus had many neat adventures
(one involved the Chimacra, whom we've heard of before).
Eventually Bellerophon got too big
for his ancient britches and tried to ride Pegasus
all the way up to Mount Olympus.
Big mistake!

Poor Bellerophon ended up wandering around alone,
while Pegasus lived happily ever after on Olympus,
carrying around Zeus's thunderbolts,
which must have been heavy.
But Pegasus didn't mind.

PHOENIX

Like a lot
of these creatures,
the phoenix was a one-of-a-kind proposition.

The phoenix was a bird
that would live to be really, really old.
  When it would turn 500, it would build a nest,
  set it on fire, and then out of the ashes would rise—
      a new phoenix!
  This new phoenix would then be good
                      for another 500 years.

The great English writer D. H. Lawrence
 was really into the phoenix concept.
  For him, as for many people,
  the phoenix meant: Immortality! Life!
And other good things.

SaLaMaNDER

A little weirdo snake-lizard kind of thing, poisonous.
Its main claim to fame was that it could
live in fire without getting burned.

Unlike the phoenix or griffin, salamanders are actually REAL—
there are little lizard-like guys called salamanders
running around in the world today.
But as for this living-in-fire bit…
forget it.

SCYLLA and CHARYBDIS

Check this out:
a six-headed
sea monster with three rows of teeth (*ouch!*) and twelve feet;
    from the waist down, Scylla consisted of twelve dogs
    THAT NEVER STOPPED BARKING. What a racket!

Scylla lived in a cave on the Italian seashore. When ships went by,
she would dart out of her cave and—*Goodbye, sailors!*
Nearby lived her pal, Charybdis, who was—maybe still is—a violent
whirlpool. *There's a charming pair!*
If Scylla didn't get you, Charybdis did—
    which is why people talk about
    being caught between Scylla and Charybdis.

And now you know.

SiRENS

Bird-women—or just plain women—
who lived on a rocky island, *singing*.
Sailors would hear their beautiful songs and freak out,
crashing their boats on the rocks.
(Hence the phrase *a siren song*:
something that lures you into MAJOR trouble.)
The great hero Odysseus
wanted to check out the songs of the Sirens,
so he asked the men in his boat
to tie him tightly to the mast of their ship.
Then he ordered his men
to put wax in their ears
and told them to keep rowing.
That way HE could hear the music
of the Sirens, suffer like crazy,
and still get where he was going.

A nice trick that every grown-up
would like to be able to perform.

SPHINX

Sphinx-like. Now what does that mean?
    It means you know something and you're not telling—
    just like the Sphinx of olden days.

What was a Sphinx, exactly?
It was a creature with a human head (man or woman, usually a woman),
the body of a lion, and—sometimes—wings.
You can see Sphinxes anywhere, everywhere—paintings of them, statues,
Sphinxes crouching on clocks, carved on jewels, etc., etc.
        Sphinxes are always kind of spooky:
                  they just sit there, silently.

Here's the main Sphinx story:
        Oedipus—a poor troubled man, roaming the earth—
        came up to the Sphinx one day and the Sphinx told Oedipus
        he'd have to answer a riddle correctly or be eaten up.
        A little nervously—you can imagine—Oedipus asked:
        What's the riddle?
        The Sphinx replied: What walks on four legs in the morning,
        two legs at noon, and three legs at night?
        Believe me, no one had been able to answer this question:
        the Sphinx had gobbled up a lot of travelers by this time.

Oedipus thought for a minute and said: I KNOW. The answer is:
A man. (Nowadays we would say a "human being," to include women,
too. Remember, this was a long time ago.)
        A man crawls around on all fours when he's a baby,
        then walks on two legs when he grows up
        and three legs when he's old. (The third leg is his cane.)

                What else could the unpleasantly surprised Sphinx
                do but say: Right you are, Oedipus!
                        And then sulk about it for a few centuries.
                (Though some people say she flipped out
                and jumped off a cliff. *Wow!*)

UNICORN

We'll end our little survey on an upbeat note, with the unicorn.
Everyone loves a unicorn!
Unicorns were horselike creatures with a long single horn
growing out from the middle of their forehead.

Unicorns became REALLY popular in the Middle Ages,
but their stories go back even further. Why were they so popular?
Maybe because they were gentle and pure—
so pure they could take the poison out of a pool or a stream
by dipping their horn in the water.
And they were secretive—it was hard to get hold of a unicorn!
In fact, so the stories go, only the fairest and purest
of ladies could even get near a unicorn.
With anyone else the unicorn would vanish, pronto.

If you're ever lucky enough to be in Paris or New York,
be sure to see the famous "Unicorn Tapestries"
in the museums there.
Woven hundreds of years ago,
they tell unicorn stories, and boy,
are they beautiful.

OK, now it's time for the MONSTER QUIZ

Can you pass it? I know I couldn't!

1. He—or she!—had a human head and the body of a lion and asked mysterious questions. It was a _____.

2. This beautiful winged horse was named _____.

3. This lizardy guy could live in fire with no problem! _____.

4. This creature was half man, half horse, and ran around in the woods. It was a _____.

5. These singing creatures lived in the sea and lured poor sailors to their doom. They were called _____.

6. This goat-guy would scare people and (hint-hint) inspired PANIC. He was known as _____.

7. This one's hard: If you're trapped in a lousy situation—between two different things, neither of which you want to do—you can say that you're caught between _____ and _____.

8. They were beautiful and had horns in the middle of their foreheads; they were _____.

9. This scary guy lived in the famous Labyrinth built for King Minos, and he was known as the _____.

10. They had snaky hair and wings and claws, and the most famous one was named Medusa. They were the _____.

How did you do? Pretty well, I bet!

Now make up your own monsters, using bits and pieces of as many animals as you can think of. The ancient Greeks and Romans did it. *Why shouldn't you!*

BONUS PRONUNCIATION GUIDE

Ariadne
air-ee-AD-nee

Bellerophon
bell-AIR-o-fon

Cerberus
SIR-ber-us

Charybdis
ka-RIB-dis

Chimaera
kye-MEER-ah

Chiron
KYE-ron

Claude Debussy
clode deb-you-see

Cyclops
SYE-clops
(Plural: Cyclopes.
Yes, *Cyclopes.*
Pronounced
sye-KLO-peez)

Faun
fawn

Hades
HAY-dees

Minos
MY-nos

Minotaur
MIN-oh-tar

Odysseus
oh-DIS-ee-us

Oedipus
ED-eh-puss

Orpheus
ORE-fee-us

Phineus
FIN-ee-us

Phoenix
FEE-nix

Polyphemus
polly-FEE-muss

Poseidon
poe-SYE-don

Satyr
SATE-er

Scylla
SILL-ah

Sphinx
sfinks

Theseus
THEE-see-us

Zeus
Zoose

For Adelaide and Beryl, who helped me write this book;
and for Rita, the fourth Angel. JH

For Adam and Seth. CB

Getty Publications
1200 Getty Center Drive, Suite 500
Los Angeles, California 90049-1682
www.getty.edu

Christopher Hudson *Publisher*
Mark Greenberg *Editor in Chief*
John Harris *Editor*
Jim Drobka *Designer*
Elizabeth Chapin Kahn *Production Coordinator*
Printed and bound by Tien Wah Press, Singapore

Library of Congress Cataloging-in-Publication Data

Harris, John, 1950 July 7–
  Greece! Rome! Monsters! / John Harris; illustrated
by Calef Brown.
    p. cm.
  ISBN 0-89236-618-4
  1. Monsters—Juvenile literature. [1. Animals,
Mythical. 2. Monsters. 3. Mythology, Greek.
4. Mythology, Roman.] I. Brown, Calef, ill. II. Title.
  GR825 .H3 2002
  398.24'54—dc21

2001002020